My Naughty Little Puppy

New Tricks for Rascal

Boing!

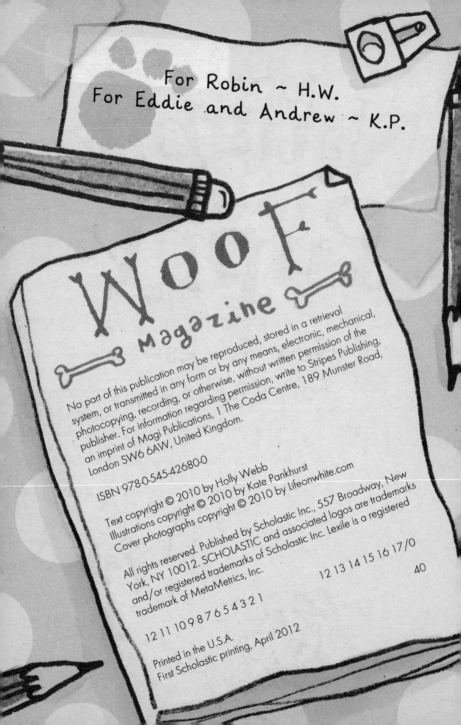

For Robin ~ H.W.
For Eddie and Andrew ~ K.P.

WOOF
magazine

ISBN 978-0-545-42680-0

Text copyright © 2010 by Holly Webb
Illustrations copyright © 2010 by Kate Pankhurst
Cover photographs copyright © 2010 by Lifeonwhite.com

12 13 14 15 16 17/0

40

12 11 10 9 8 7 6 5 4 3 2 1

Printed in the U.S.A.
First Scholastic printing, April 2012

My Naughty Little Puppy

New Tricks for Rascal

Holly Webb

Illustrated by
Kate Pankhurst

SCHOLASTIC INC.

New York   Toronto   London   Auckland
Sydney   Mexico City   New Delhi   Hong Kong

Chapter One

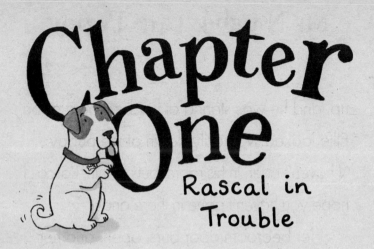

Rascal in Trouble

"Ellie! ELLIE!"

Ellie jumped, losing her place in the book she was reading. Max was yelling and he sounded furious.

She heard Max's bedroom door bang and then the sound of him thundering across the landing. "I haven't even been in his room," she muttered to Rascal, who was lying on the bed next to her while she read her book for school. Rascal's ears were pricked

My Naughty Little Puppy

up, and he was staring at her bedroom door.
Ellie looked worriedly down at the puppy.
"*I* haven't been in his room, but . . . Oh, Rascal, I
hope you haven't gone in there and—"

Her bedroom door burst open, and her
brother marched in, his face bright red with
anger. He was waving something
black and white and squished-
looking at her. "Look!"

My Naughty Little Puppy

"What is it?" Ellie's voice wobbled. Max
was ten, two years older than she was, and
he was usually very easygoing. But when he
was angry, he could be really scary.

"You see! You can't even tell what it is!
Because that stupid dog chewed it! It's my
soccer ball, Ellie! The one autographed by
the team, that I waited for three hours
to get!" Max chucked the ball on the floor.
"Or it was. It's just garbage now."

"I'm really sorry." Ellie felt her eyes filling
with tears. "Did you leave your bedroom
door open?"

"Don't try and make this my fault!" Max
yelled. "It's your dog that ruined it! I'm going
to tell Mom, and you know what, Ellie? I'm
going to say we should send Rascal back

to the dog breeder. He's the worst-behaved puppy in the world!"

Max stormed out, and Ellie watched him go, horrified.

Rascal whimpered, frightened by the shouting, and Ellie hugged him tight. "He didn't mean it," she whispered. "And Mom and Dad would never send you back."

But as she heard Max downstairs, telling Mom about why Rascal should go back to the breeder's, and Mom answer that she would think about it, Ellie didn't feel quite so sure.

The next morning, Ellie sat at the bottom of the stairs, pulling on her school shoes.

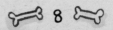

My Naughty Little Puppy

She wriggled her toes sadly. These shoes weren't nearly as comfy as the sneakers she'd worn all through spring break. The time off seemed to have gone so quickly, with all the excitement of getting their new puppy.

Rascal sniffed at her feet curiously, and nibbled the end of the Velcro strap with his sharp little white teeth.

Ellie gently pushed him off. "No, Rascal! Mom will go crazy if you eat my school shoes. You ate half of her sock yesterday, remember? And she still hasn't forgiven you for chewing her sneakers."

Rascal looked up at Ellie, his eyes sparkling with mischief. There was just something about shoes!

My Naughty Little Puppy

"Are you ready, Ellie?" Mom asked, coming downstairs. Max and Ellie usually walked together. Their big sister, Lila, went in the other direction to go to her middle school.

"Can you come, too, so we can bring Rascal?" Ellie asked Mom hopefully as she got to her feet. "I bet he'd love a walk. He's going to miss us."

"*I'm* not going to miss him," Max growled as he stomped down the stairs. He was still really angry with Rascal.

Rascal had heard the word *walk* and was dancing around underneath the hook where his leash hung, barking excitedly.

"Oh, please . . ." Ellie begged. "Look at him, Mom!"

"Not now. Look at the time! You're going to be late if you don't hurry. But I'll bring him to meet you after school, okay?"

Ellie's best friend, Christy, was waiting for her outside the school. "Oh, I was hoping you'd have Rascal!" she said when she saw Ellie and Max running down the road.

"Mom said no, because we were late." Ellie panted. "But she's bringing him this afternoon so I can show him off to everyone!"

She told Christy all about Rascal and Max's soccer ball as they were putting their bags away in the classroom. "He still isn't talking to me—he didn't say one word all the way to school. And last night when Max said we should send Rascal back, Mom said she would think about it! Then Dad went out in the yard later and found this huge hole in the lawn. . . ."

"Settle down, please, everyone!" Mrs. Harley, Ellie's teacher, looked over at her and Christy. "Less chatting, Ellie. Your vocabulary words are up on the board."

"Sorry," Ellie muttered, turning red. She didn't usually get reprimanded at school. But she cheered up later, when Mrs. Harley asked anyone who'd done something exciting over the break to share it with the class. Ellie raised her hand. Sometimes she was shy about speaking up in front of people, but she wanted everyone to know about Rascal.

"Yes, Ellie?" said Mrs. Harley.

"We got a puppy last week. His name's Rascal."

"That's exciting." Mrs. Harley smiled at her. "What kind of dog is he?"

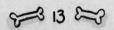

"A Jack Russell terrier. He's thirteen weeks old. My mom's bringing him when she comes to pick me up, if you want to see him."

Mrs. Harley nodded. "I'd love to."

At recess, lots of people from Ellie's class asked her about Rascal. She just couldn't wait to show him off. But she was a little worried, too.

Christy nudged her as they sat back at their desks. "Are you okay?"

Ellie leaned closer to whisper. She didn't want Mrs. Harley to get mad again. "I'm just worried about Rascal. I hope he's not being naughty at home. Last time I left him, he howled the whole time."

"Your mom's there, isn't she?"

Ellie nodded. "But he misses *me*!" She

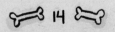

couldn't help feeling a little glow of pride
at that.

Mom looked frazzled when she came
to meet Ellie and Max. She was standing
outside, holding Rascal's leash very tightly.
She tried to get him to shush as he started
barking at a stroller.

"Hi, Mom! Has Rascal been okay?" Ellie
asked, crouching down to say hello to him.
Rascal bounced up and down, trying to lick
her face.

Mom sighed. "He howled all day. I
could hardly get any work done. And look
at his leash! He pulled it down off the hook
and chewed it to pieces!"

My Naughty Little Puppy

"Oh, no!" Ellie took the red leash from her mom. It was now chewed all down one side!

Just then, Christy rushed over. "Hello, Rascal!" she said, bending down and tickling him. The puppy frisked around her, his whole body wagging with his tail. Other girls from Ellie's class crowded around to take turns petting him, too.

Ellie saw Mrs. Harley coming over. "He's lovely, Ellie." She bent down to pet the lively puppy, and he jumped up at her, yapping happily.

It was only when he turned around to be petted by one of the other girls that Ellie noticed the trail of little muddy paw prints down Mrs. Harley's beautiful pale pink skirt. . . .

My Naughty Little Puppy

Ellie flushed pink. "Oh, I'm so sorry, Mrs. Harley—I didn't see he was muddy!"

Mrs. Harley smiled. "Don't worry, it'll wash off. My dog's always doing that."

Ellie nodded, but she still felt embarrassed, and Mom hurried them away from school before Rascal caused any more trouble.

On the walk home, Rascal sniffed every fence and lamppost, and soon he and Ellie were way behind Mom and Max.

"Come on!" Mom called. "I guess it's good at least that he's walking now," she said with a sigh when Ellie caught up. "I had to carry him most of the way to school!"

Chapter Two

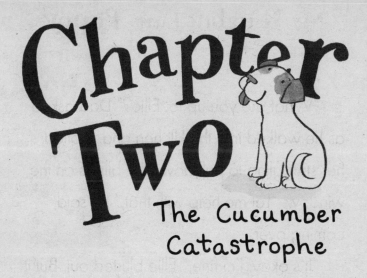

The Cucumber Catastrophe

That evening, Ellie was struggling with her science homework at the kitchen table when she suddenly had a thought. She'd let Rascal out to do his business earlier, and he'd been in the yard for an awfully long time. She jumped up and ran to the window. She could just see a small white shape scrabbling away—in the middle of Dad's vegetable garden.

At that moment, she heard the front door open. Dad was home!

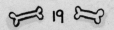

My Naughty Little Puppy

"What are you up to, Ellie?" Dad asked
as he walked into the kitchen and spotted
her struggling to pull down the blinds on the
window. "Let me help with that," he said,
coming over.

"It's okay, I'm fine," Ellie blurted out. But it
was too late. . . .

"Have you seen what he's doing?" Dad
yelled as he spotted Rascal through the
window. He flung open the
back door and raced down
the path.

Ellie watched anxiously
as Dad grabbed Rascal
and stomped back indoors
with the puppy tucked under
his arm.

My Naughty Little Puppy

"He dug up every single one of my cucumber seedlings! I only planted them outside yesterday!" Dad snapped.

"Sorry," Ellie whispered. "He just likes digging. He doesn't understand. . . ."

Dad put Rascal down, and the puppy cowered under Ellie's chair.

"I know, Ellie. But he can't be allowed to dig everything up."

"He hasn't had as many walks today as usual, because I was at school," Ellie explained. "He was working off all his energy."

"We'll talk about this later," Dad said, and stormed off.

Ellie looked down at Rascal, who was sitting under her chair. "What are we going

My Naughty Little Puppy

to do, Rascal? Now Mom, Dad, *and* Max are all angry with you."

Just then, Max came into the kitchen. He crouched down next to Rascal and held out his hand solemnly. "Shake a paw, Rascal. All is forgiven."

"What are you doing?" Ellie asked as Rascal licked Max's hand instead.

"He dug up all of Dad's cucumbers, Ellie! I *hate* cucumbers! Do you think you could get him to work on the beets next?"

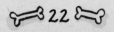

My Naughty Little Puppy

At least Max wasn't mad at Ellie and Rascal anymore. But Dad had a serious talk with Ellie that night, and Ellie was starting to feel worried. What if Mom and Dad *did* decide that Rascal was too naughty? Would they really send him back, like Max had said? She knew that Rascal had already had another home before they got him, with an elderly couple who'd found him to be too much of a handful.

"You're only a little bit naughty," Ellie told Rascal as she brushed him out in the yard after school the next day. She'd noticed a lot of white hairs around the house, and she didn't want Mom and Dad to have anything else to be grumpy with Rascal about.

But as she let Rascal back into the

kitchen and put the grooming brush away,
Ellie heard a howl of horror from upstairs.

Mom looked up from the vegetables she
was chopping. "Was that Lila?"

Ellie stared down at Rascal. "Please
tell me that's not because of you!" she
whispered.

About ten seconds later, Lila burst into the
kitchen. Her eyes were glittering with fury,
and she pointed at Rascal, who backed
behind Ellie.

"He ate my new pink lipstick!"

Ellie's eyes widened. "Oh, no—"

"And *then*," Lila went on, "he got sick all
over my carpet!"

Ellie felt a terrible urge to giggle. It was
awful, but funny at the same time.

"I'll clean it up," she volunteered, hoping that might make Lila feel better. "And I'll buy you new lipstick." She gave a sigh. She had wanted to use her allowance to buy Rascal a squeaky bone toy to distract him from digging.

My Naughty Little Puppy

"Clean it up together," Mom said. "And please be quick, girls. Your granddad's coming over for dinner, remember?"

Lila grabbed the carpet cleaner and headed upstairs, muttering about horrible, smelly dogs. Ellie set off after Lila, closing the kitchen door firmly as Rascal tried to follow. Rascal gave a hurt little whimper, but Ellie didn't give in. He definitely wouldn't be welcome in Lila's room!

Mom passed Granddad a slice of cake, and gave him a serious look. "Do you have any ideas for how we can get Rascal to behave, Dad? He's turning into a nightmare."

Granddad bit into his cake and looked

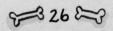

over at Rascal, who was sitting next to Ellie's chair and eyeing her portion hopefully.

"Jack Russells can be tricky. They're really determined, which is what makes them such little characters, but it means it's hard to train them. I think you might need some help. Have you thought about puppy-training classes?"

My Naughty Little Puppy

Ellie smiled at Granddad. Puppy-training classes sounded like a great idea!

But Mom looked thoughtful. "Isn't he a little young for that? I'd planned to take him to some over the summer."

Granddad shook his head. "No, not at all. The younger the better. Lots of classes have puppy time, when they just let the pups play together. That's really important for helping him get him used to other dogs, too."

"Rascal always barks at other dogs in the park," Ellie added. "Even if they're twice as big as he is!"

"I'll check online later and see if there are any local classes." Dad looked pleased. "But I think we all have to make a real effort to help Rascal behave, too. Like making sure we don't leave things lying around for him to chew."

"And remembering to keep your doors shut!" Mom added.

Max made a grumpy noise through a mouthful of cake.

"And he needs more exercise and lots of fun play," Dad went on. "Puppy training isn't going to stop him from getting bored and digging holes, is it?"

Lila shrugged. "He's Ellie's dog, so shouldn't she be doing all of that?"

Ellie beamed. She wouldn't mind that at all!

Chapter Three

The Dog-Training Disaster

With Ellie's help, Dad found a website advertising dog-training classes nearby. He called the instructor later that evening and signed Rascal up to start soon. Luckily, there was a space in her beginners' class, which began on Friday, so they could start that very week.

Ellie was so excited. "Can I please come with you, Dad?" she begged as soon as he got off the phone.

My Naughty Little Puppy

Dad laughed. "You *have* to come!
You're the only one who can get him to
behave. If it was only me, he'd probably just
decide to lie down and sulk!"

Ellie giggled, but it was true. And it was
a little bit worrying. What if Rascal didn't behave
for her, either? She frowned. That couldn't be
allowed to happen. Mom and Dad already
thought Rascal was a problem dog. He had to
be a star at puppy-training class and prove that
he was good enough to stay.

Ellie lay in bed that night with Rascal
curled up on her feet. (Mom had given up
trying to get him to sleep in the kitchen.) She
was in that dreamy, half-asleep state, and
pictures of Rascal trotting perfectly to heel
flitted through her mind. She also imagined

Rascal sitting when she told him to—instead of looking at her with a *Why?* face, like he did now. And Rascal fetching Dad's slippers . . . Ellie giggled. Maybe not. The slippers would definitely be full of holes when Rascal finished with them!

"Rascal, we're going somewhere really exciting today." Ellie was sitting on the living-room floor with Rascal after school on Friday, watching TV. "And you have to be very, very good, okay?"

Lila leaned over from the sofa. "Ellie, why are you talking to the dog?"

Max snickered. "She thinks he understands."

My Naughty Little Puppy

"He does!" Ellie protested. She looked down at Rascal, who was staring at her with bright, smart eyes. She was sure he understood her serious tone of voice, anyway.

Ellie had already packed a bag with Rascal's favorite chew toy, the chicken-flavored treats he really liked, a bottle of water, his bowl, and some plastic bags in case he had an accident. She kept checking it, worrying that she'd forgotten something.

They set off as soon as Dad got home. That way they could fit in a quick run around the park first, so that Rascal wouldn't be too lively during the class—and had a chance to go to the bathroom beforehand. But Ellie's nervous feeling only got worse as she and Dad got to

My Naughty Little Puppy

the class and saw all the other puppies and owners.

Ellie spotted a girl with a neat bob, who she recognized, also going inside. "Oh! That's a girl from my school," Ellie whispered. "Amelia. She's in fifth grade."

She had never spoken to Amelia, who was in the same class as Max, but she knew Max had said she was stuck-up. Amelia was with her mom, and they had a beautiful King Charles spaniel with huge, fluffy ears. Ellie wouldn't have been surprised if Amelia had blow-dried them for him.

"That's nice," Dad said.

Ellie looked horrified. "No, it isn't! What if we do it all wrong and she tells everyone at school?"

"I'm sure it will be fine," Dad said.

Unfortunately, he was wrong. As Ellie led Rascal into the hall, he dashed forward, dragging Ellie along behind him.

"Come back, Rascal!" Ellie muttered, going red as everyone turned around to stare. But Rascal got overexcited by being around so many puppies at once, and he barked himself silly, jumping up and down and running in circles.

"Pick him up, Ellie," Dad hissed.

Ellie hugged Rascal tightly and tried to calm him down, but he kept yapping and trying to wriggle out of her arms.

My Naughty Little Puppy

"Don't worry." The instructor, Jo, came over to them, smiling. She was much younger than Ellie had imagined she'd be, with a long brown braid. "He'll get used to it soon. This is Rascal, isn't it? We're just going to start with everyone introducing themselves."

She gathered them all together, and Ellie looked around curiously at the other dogs. Rascal was definitely the smallest, but they

My Naughty Little Puppy

all looked young. Along with Amelia and
her dog, Goldie, there was a chocolate
Labrador puppy named Sam; a Dalmatian
named Libby; a Westie, Angus, who was
almost as small as Rascal; and Josh, a
border collie pup. Jo had brought her
own dog, too, a beautiful yellow Labrador
named Emma, who looked like she knew
everything there was to know about
dog training.

My Naughty Little Puppy

"These classes are all about you ending up with a happy, well-behaved dog," Jo explained. "A dog who gets along well with your family, and with other dogs, too. So, we're going to start with some playtime. I think we'll put Libby, Sam, and Josh together in one group. Then Angus, Goldie, and Rascal in the other, since they're about the same size."

Jo moved the two groups to opposite ends of the room, and told all the owners to crouch down. "That way your puppy knows you're nice and close if he's scared. We'll take their leashes off and let them play with these rope toys. If one of the pups starts being too rough, just gently take them away for a minute, okay?"

Ellie undid Rascal's leash. He looked

My Naughty Little Puppy

up at her curiously, and then went to sniff
the rope. But Angus wanted it, too, and as
he tugged it away Rascal barked loudly.
Everyone in the hall turned around to look.

Goldie had been sitting watching, but
now she tried to join in, and Rascal noticed
her for the first time. He trotted over and
started trying to sniff her bottom!

My Naughty Little Puppy

"Stop him!" Amelia snapped. Ellie
snatched him up, her face scarlet. After
that, Goldie and Amelia kept giving Rascal
identical disgusted looks, and Ellie felt like a
worm. She was glad when Jo told everyone
to put the puppies' leashes back on, so they
could practice walking to heel.

"Get your treats out, everyone.
Remember, we want the dogs to enjoy
training, and to want to do what they're told.
So, when your dog is paying attention to
you, reward him. When he's walking, have
the treat just in front of his nose, so he follows
along. Here we go." Jo got them all walking
in a circle around the room.

Rascal's tail was wagging as he
followed his favorite treat, and he looked

like he was enjoying himself. Ellie took a deep, relieved breath. He finally seemed to be been getting used to this training thing!

Then Rascal bolted, pulling the leash out of her hand. Ellie squeaked and chased after him.

Rascal whizzed up the stairs to the stage, where everyone had left their bags, and Ellie gasped. She knew what he was doing. Jo ran lots of classes that evening, and she'd mentioned that she brought sandwiches to keep her going.

Delicious-looking chicken sandwiches, one of which was now hanging out of Rascal's mouth.

Chapter Four

A Bigger Dog-Training Disaster

"That's her, over there." Ellie pointed across the playground.

Christy stared at the group of gossiping fifth-grade girls. "Oh, *her*! I know who you mean now. Poor you!" Christy giggled. "I can just imagine Rascal sniffing her dog's bottom. . . ."

"It was awful," Ellie muttered. "The whole class. I've been thinking about it all weekend. Jo said it didn't matter about the sandwich, but I was so embarrassed, and Dad almost made us go home before it was over."

"Your dad's got a couple of days to get over it before the next class, right?"

"The next class is tomorrow. Tuesdays and Fridays. I just have to try to avoid Amelia till then," Ellie added, hiding behind Christy as Amelia glanced their way.

"Rascal will get it in the end," Christy promised. "I know he will."

Ellie frowned. "He's still being a monster while I'm at school, too. I'm really worried Mom and Dad are going to say he's too much for us. That's why it's so important that he's good at the training. And at the end of the lesson, Jo told us there's going to be a show at the last class."

My Naughty Little Puppy

"They did that at Bouncer's classes. He came in second place," Christy said proudly.

"Well, right now, Rascal would be in about millionth place, and there are only six dogs in the class," Ellie said gloomily.

"Maybe you could teach him something really special," Christy suggested. "Like a trick that no one else knows. That would show everyone."

Ellie nodded thoughtfully. Now all she had to do was come up with the perfect trick.

On Tuesday, Ellie and Dad arrived at the class at the same time as a boy about Ellie's age, who was leading the biggest dog Ellie had ever seen. His mom was

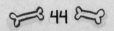

hurrying along behind them.

"Sorry!" the boy gasped to Ellie as the enormous black-and-white creature squished him and Ellie together in the doorway. "Can't stop him!"

"Wow," Dad muttered. "That's a dog and a half."

The dog stopped just inside the door, and the boy apologized to Ellie again.

"He's so big! What kind of dog is he?" Ellie asked.

"He's a Great Dane," the boy said proudly. "He's named Hugo—because he's huge! And I'm Jack. We just adopted him from the dog shelter."

"I'm Ellie, and this is Rascal. Is this the first time you've been to puppy training?"

My Naughty Little Puppy

Jack nodded. "Yup. We were supposed to come on Friday, but we had to go to the vet's instead." He went red. "Hugo ate one of my socks."

Ellie giggled. "Rascal does that! And he chews shoes. We'd better not let them gang up."

Rascal and Hugo were already giving each other interested sniffs. Hugo was so giant that Rascal could fit underneath him with room to spare.

My Naughty Little Puppy

"Is the training difficult?" Jack asked nervously. "Hugo isn't very good at doing what he's told, and he's so big he just pulls me after him." Then he gave Ellie a fierce sort of look. "But I don't care. He's an awesome dog, and I wasn't going to leave him in that shelter without anyone to love him."

Ellie nodded firmly. "I think he's great," she said encouragingly. "Look how nice he's being with Rascal." Then she sighed. "Honestly, you can't be worse than we are. Look, my dad's so embarrassed, he's hiding at the back."

Jack chuckled, but then he looked anxious again as Jo called everyone to begin the class.

It helped a little that Ellie knew what to

expect, but Rascal didn't seem to have improved, even though she'd practiced with him over the weekend. At least Amelia gave her disgusted look to both Ellie *and* Jack this time. Hugo was so big that if he went the wrong way, everyone knew about it.

"Let's do the 'sit' command now," Jo called near the end. "Hold the treat over the puppy's nose, and move it back so your pup naturally sits down. Say 'sit' clearly and firmly as he sits, and reward him with the treat."

Ellie frowned. Jo made it sound so simple. Rascal wagged his tail delightedly as she got out the treats. She held one carefully over his nose, and started to move it back.

For a second it looked like it was about

My Naughty Little Puppy

to work, and then Rascal fell over backward.
He bounced up again with a confused little
"Woof!" and Ellie heard Amelia tittering.
Goldie was sitting perfectly, of course.

Jack held his treat over Hugo's nose,
but he had to reach up to do it because
Hugo was so tall. Hugo wagged his tail
enthusiastically and simply ate the treat out
of Jack's hand. Amelia giggled again.

"Lots of practice is the key thing," Jo told them encouragingly. "Just five minutes, two or three times a day. They'll get there. Now, does anyone have any behavior problems they want to talk about before the end of the session?"

Ellie looked down at Rascal. He'd done so many naughty things recently, she wasn't sure where to start. But then Ellie remembered how Rascal was still howling whenever she left him, and how Mom was hardly getting any work done. She looked around nervously, wishing somebody else would go first, but everyone was silent.

"Um, Jo?" She waved a hand. "Rascal barks and whines a lot while I'm at school. It drives my mom crazy!"

Jo looked thoughtful. "Have you tried putting one of your shirts in his basket?" she asked. "Jack Russells can be very devoted to one owner, and if he thinks he's taking care of something for you, he might be happier when you're gone."

Ellie smiled. "Thanks, Jo."

"No problem. See you all on Friday," Jo called, and everyone started to gather their things.

Amelia walked past Jack and Ellie, smirking. "Bet you're glad you've found another dog that's as useless as yours," she said, sneering as she made for the door.

Ellie gasped, and Jack's mouth dropped open. "What's with her?" he said at last.

My Naughty Little Puppy

Ellie shook her head and smiled at him.
"She's just a mean girl from my school.
Rascal and Hugo are going to be amazing
by the end of the course."

Behind her back, Ellie had her fingers
crossed.

Chapter Five

Ice Cream for Rascal

"So did Jo's tip about your shirt work?"
Christy asked. It was Saturday, and Ellie and
her mom were having a picnic in the park
with Christy, her mom, and Christy's little
sister, Jade.

Ellie nodded. "Yes! I gave Rascal my
old pink hoodie, and Mom says he hardly
whines at all now! Jo's so smart. I said thank
you to her at the class on Friday and asked
if she had any more tips for Rascal. She said

it was just all about working with the dog and finding their strengths." Ellie sighed. "But I'm not sure what his strengths are, apart from guarding pink hoodies! I wish he was getting better at the rest of his training, too."

Christy nodded. "But Bouncer took forever to pick up his training," she pointed out, scratching Bouncer's ears. "Didn't you, boy? And he's a Lab—they're supposed to be good at it! I'm sure Rascal will get there."

Ellie stared at Rascal, flat out on his back on the grass, with his paws in the air. "I hope so. I still need to find a special trick to teach him, just to show everyone how smart he is. He *is* smart, you know. He must be, to think up so many ways to be naughty. . . ."

My Naughty Little Puppy

"Girls, would you like some ice cream?" Christy's mom called.

"Ooh, yes, please!" they answered.

Everyone got up to stroll over to the ice cream truck, and Rascal perked up at the sight of food. As the girls took their ice creams, Rascal wagged his tail eagerly.

"I can't, Rascal," Ellie whispered. "Mom's watching!" Ellie's mom was very strict about not giving him anything that wasn't his dog food.

"You wouldn't like it anyway, Rascal," Christy told him. "It makes your teeth cold."

But Rascal continued to wag his tail hopefully. He couldn't reach Ellie's ice cream, or Christy's, but there was another one very close to his nose.

My Naughty Little Puppy

Christy's three-year-old sister, Jade, was wandering slowly back to the picnic blanket. Her ice cream was dripping temptingly.

As Ellie took another lick of her cone, Rascal suddenly pulled the leash from her grip. He then whipped around and snatched the ice cream out of Jade's hand.

My Naughty Little Puppy

"Heyyyy!" Jade wailed as Rascal bounded off. "My ice cream! He took my iiiiice cream!" And she started to howl, even louder than Rascal could.

"I'm sorry, Jade! Please don't cry. We'll get you another one," Ellie promised.

Ellie's mom hurried over, looking horrified. "Ellie! How could you let him do that?"

Mom gave Ellie the money to get another ice cream, and took Rascal's leash while Ellie hurried off. Meanwhile, Rascal was busily licking up his stolen ice cream, slurping it out of the cone with big swipes of his pink tongue. He shivered deliciously as he finished it. Then he picked up the cone delicately in his teeth, and offered it back to Jade.

Jade shook her head.

"Ugh, no, Rascal!" Ellie said as she returned with the new ice cream and took his leash back from Mom.

Jade started to laugh. "He doesn't like cones! *I* don't like the cones, either!" She giggled.

Ellie couldn't help laughing with her. At least Jade wasn't upset anymore. But Mom still seemed furious.

Chapter Six

The Roast-Chicken Incident

"We need to do something amazing to show Mom you're a genius dog," Ellie told Rascal as she took him into the yard on Sunday morning. She wanted to try out the trick she'd found in one of her dog magazines. "Believe me, Rascal, we've got a lot of making up to do. You are not Mom's favorite pet right now. And we only *have* one pet! I still can't believe she made me pay her back for Jade's ice cream out of

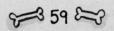

my allowance yesterday. I don't know how
I'm ever going to be able to save up to get
you a new leash before the dog show."

Rascal watched with his head to one
side as Ellie took a dog treat out of a packet.
"Look, Rascal. Your favorite chicken treats!"

Rascal gave an eager little whine.

Ellie carefully put the treat on his nose.
"Don't eat it! I said *don't* eat it. . . . Oh well.
Let's try again."

My Naughty Little Puppy

Rascal licked his chops as Ellie placed another treat on his nose. This was a good game! He was almost cross-eyed trying to see it, and his tongue was creeping out of his mouth.

"No, no, wait till I say! Oh." The treat had already disappeared, and Rascal was watching her eagerly for more. Ellie sighed. "I suppose we just need to keep practicing."

Mom was just about to start preparing Sunday dinner, and had called Max, Lila, and Ellie into the kitchen. "You will all behave beautifully, okay?" she told them. "This is the first time Aunt Jenna is bringing her new boyfriend over."

My Naughty Little Puppy

"Yes, Mom." Max rolled his eyes.

"What's his name again?" Lila asked.

"Liam. And please make sure the dog behaves, too," Mom added.

Ellie nodded frantically.

"Now, it would really help if you could all stay out of the kitchen while I make the chicken."

Ellie slipped out into the yard with Rascal and his grooming brush, and the dog treats. She was determined to get the trick right eventually.

"I'm sure you kept it on your nose longer that time," Ellie murmured as Rascal gobbled down another treat. "Let's take a break. Should I make you look beautiful?" She started to brush Rascal lovingly, making sure his white coat gleamed. "We need to show

My Naughty Little Puppy

you off to Aunt Jenna and Liam."

Just then, Mom called, "Come in, please, Ellie. They'll be here in a minute. Oh, Ellie." She sighed. "Look at you, you're covered in dog hair! Go and change. I need to change, too, actually." Mom looked down at her apron. "The chicken can just stay on the counter and rest. Dinner is all ready, except for the roasted potatoes."

My Naughty Little Puppy

"It smells great." Ellie sniffed the delicious roast-chicken smell as she headed out of the kitchen. Mom was obviously making a big effort for this Sunday dinner.

Ellie went upstairs to change her top. She was just coming back down when the doorbell rang. "I'll get it!" she called.

Aunt Jenna was standing at the door with a nice-looking, dark-haired man who seemed a bit nervous.

"Hi, Ellie! Liam, this is one of my nieces. Ellie's the one who really loves dogs."

Liam smiled at Ellie. "Jenna tells me you just got a puppy."

Ellie nodded shyly. "Yes, his name is Rascal."

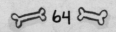

My Naughty Little Puppy

Dad popped his head out of the living room to say hello, and Mom hurried downstairs. "Hi, Jenna. It's great to meet you, Liam. I've just got to run to the kitchen— dinner is almost ready!" She disappeared into the kitchen. Then there was a sudden scuffling noise, and everyone in the hallway clearly heard Mom shriek, "Oh, no! Bad dog!"

"What is it?" Ellie cried, dashing after her.

But as soon as she got into the kitchen, she could see. Rascal was sitting at the bottom of the step stool Mom used for the high cupboards, looking really guilty. And in his mouth was what was left of the chicken.

My Naughty Little Puppy

"Honestly, I really do love fish sticks," Liam told Ellie's mom. "*And* they're delicious with gravy."

Mom smiled, but she still looked really upset.

Ellie felt so guilty that she hardly spoke during dinner. She knew how hard Mom had worked on the meal, and then Rascal had gone and ruined it. At least he hadn't gotten anywhere near the dessert, which was an enormous chocolate cake.

Mom had banished Rascal to the yard, and now Ellie could hear him whimpering and scratching at the back door as she helped with the dishes.

My Naughty Little Puppy

"I guess you'd better let him in." Mom sighed.

"I'm really sorry," Ellie whispered.

Mom gave her a hug. "I know. And it's my fault, anyway. I've told all of you so many times not to leave anything where Rascal can get it. I just didn't think about him climbing the step stool!"

"He's a master criminal!" Ellie said, opening the back door for Rascal. But he didn't look like a master criminal. He looked lonely and miserable, as if he'd hated being shut outside. He slunk through the door with his tail between his legs.

"Oh, dear, now I feel guilty," Mom said sadly.

Ellie shook her head. "He was really

My Naughty Little Puppy

naughty, Mom. I think Liam likes dogs, though. Can I go and show him Rascal?"

Mom nodded, and Ellie called Rascal to follow her into the living room.

"Here, boy!" Liam reached down to pet Rascal, and Rascal beat his tail on the floor, sitting happily at Liam's feet.

Ellie gave a sigh of relief. Maybe Rascal was going to make up for the chicken incident.

"So, how old is he?" Liam asked, tickling Rascal behind the ears.

"About three months—" Ellie started to say, but then she broke off. "Rascal? What's wrong?"

Rascal was making strange coughing noises, and his little shoulders were heaving.

"Oh, no! The chicken!" Ellie squeaked.

"Liam, move your feet!" Max yelled.

But it was too late. Ellie gasped in horror as Rascal gave one more huge cough and threw up the stolen chicken all over Aunt Jenna's new boyfriend's feet.

Chapter Seven

The New and Improved Rascal?

Ellie was feeling really hopeful about Tuesday's class. She had been making a big effort with Rascal to try to make things up to Mom after the disastrous Sunday dinner. Whenever she had a spare moment, she walked Rascal to heel, and practiced "sit," "down," and "stay." And she'd been working on their special new trick. Rascal still ate the treat before he was told, but at least he seemed to know he wasn't supposed to, which was a start.

So her heart wasn't thumping quite as fast as usual when she and Dad and Rascal walked into the training class. Jack waved to her, and Hugo swung his thick tail joyfully as he spotted his friend Rascal.

"Let's start with our 'heeling,'" Jo called as the owners and their puppies got in line. "I think everyone's getting this now, aren't you? Great job, Jack and Hugo!"

Ellie watched enviously as Hugo paced around the hall at Jack's side. He looked so grand and solemn, as though he was thinking carefully about every footstep.

She set off, hoping that they would do just as well. But Rascal wasn't in a serious mood at all. He was bright, bouncy, and full of energy. Instead of walking calmly on a loose leash, watching Ellie for his treat, like he was supposed to, he was twirling and scampering around her. Ellie had to keep calling him back to his place.

"Ellie, don't get frustrated with him. You're doing well," Jo called. But Ellie felt like crying. Like Jo had said, everyone else was getting it right, but Rascal was worse than ever. How could he be so silly now, when he'd been doing so well during their practice?

Suddenly, Rascal darted around her legs again, and Ellie's eyes were so blurred with tears that she tripped over his leash.

Ellie landed with a thump. "Ow," she cried as she hit her elbow hard on the floor.

Dad hurried over. "Ellie, are you okay?"

Ellie nodded, but her elbow ached horribly.

Rascal crept over to her, looking guilty. He gave Ellie's hand a lick, as if to say sorry, and then he nosed at Ellie lovingly.

"That dog is so useless," Ellie heard someone say, and she glanced up to see Amelia talking to her mother.

 73

My Naughty Little Puppy

Ellie rubbed her sleeve over her eyes. They thought her adorable Rascal was *useless*.

"Oh, Ellie! You really went down hard there," said Jo, coming over to check on her. "Are you hurt?"

"Not really," Ellie muttered, struggling up with Dad's help, "I just banged my elbow."

"You sit down and rest," Dad said. "I'll take over for a bit."

Rascal looked confused when Dad took his leash. He sat down, pulling back on the leash and staring at Ellie.

"Go on, Rascal." Ellie nodded to him, and reluctantly he got up to follow Dad.

Ellie sat in the corner and watched Dad with Rascal. They were supposed to be practicing "sit," but Rascal wasn't really watching the treats that Dad was holding over his nose. He would sit nicely, but then spring up to look over at Ellie.

Jo came to talk to Ellie again at the end of the class, crouching down beside her.

My Naughty Little Puppy

"How's your elbow?"

"Fine," Ellie muttered. She felt so bad —and the worst thing was that she'd really thought Rascal would be better this week.

"Ellie, I know you're finding it difficult with Rascal right now, but he will improve, I promise you. What's great is that you haven't given up, and you're still being patient with him. I can tell you've been practicing, too. That's really good. You should be very proud of her," she added to Dad.

Ellie managed a very small smile. Jo was being so nice, but Ellie wasn't sure she believed her.

Maybe Amelia was right about Rascal.

Chapter Eight

Ellie Downhearted

"You can't give up!" cried Christy. It was morning recess on Wednesday, the day after Ellie's awful class, and she had just finished telling Christy the whole terrible story.

"Haven't you been listening?" Ellie thumped her hand on the arm of the bench they were sitting on. "Ow. That hurt. Amelia was right, Christy. Rascal was useless. He wouldn't follow any of the commands

correctly, and he made me look totally
stupid in front of everyone." She shuddered.
"I don't even want to think about the show."

"So that's it?" Christy looked horrified.
"You're going to stop training him?"

"I'm not *training* him!" Ellie said wearily.
"I'm just being dragged all over the place
by him!"

Ellie heard the sound of someone laughing
and looked up to see Amelia walking toward
the bench. "I'm so glad you're giving up,
Ellie. Saves me some trouble. I was coming
to tell you that you should really stop puppy-
training class, because you're just ruining it for
everyone else."

"I'm not," Ellie said, but then her voice
wavered. She gulped and blinked back

her tears. She would *not* let Amelia make her cry.

"You waste Jo's time when she ought to be helping the others," Amelia went on.

"That's what training's *for*," Christy snapped. "Dogs who actually need it. If you're so perfect, why are you in the beginners' class?"

"Goldie is a beginner, too, but she does what she's told. That little rat of Ellie's is never going to learn anything."

Ellie bounced up. "Rascal is not a rat! He's a beautiful dog, and you're just *mean!*"

"Yeah, Rascal is adorable, and smart, too," Christy put in. She grabbed Ellie's hand and squeezed it.

Luckily, the bell rang just then, and Amelia turned on her heel and stalked away.

But as they walked back into class, Ellie was pink-cheeked with fury. "I'm not giving up now," she told Christy. "We're going to show her. I *will* get Rascal to learn, even if we have to practice every minute of the day!"

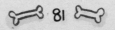

My Naughty Little Puppy

Mom brought Rascal to meet Ellie and Max after school, and Ellie made an extra-special fuss over him. Christy joined in, too. Then Jessie and Lydia from their class came over and wanted to pet him, and Rascal started to get really excited, jumping and yapping and scrabbling at their legs.

Ellie asked Mom to pass her the packet of Rascal's special treats. "Sit," she said firmly, holding a treat above his nose. And he did! Rascal stopped yapping and sat beautifully for the girls to pet him.

"Good boy!" Ellie was so pleased she felt like giving him the whole packet.

Christy rolled her eyes. "I thought he

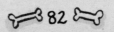

hadn't learned anything, and you wanted to give up?"

Mom overheard. "Ellie! You can't! You've done so well with him. He walked to school beautifully, even when one of those big trucks he usually barks his head off at drove past."

"See?" Christy nudged her.

Ellie nodded. "I guess it's been happening gradually and I haven't noticed. But he really was terrible in yesterday's lesson."

"Everyone can have bad days," Mom said firmly. "It's just a pity you'll have to miss the next class."

Ellie looked up at her in horror. "What do you mean?"

"Oh, Ellie." Mom sighed. "Didn't you listen to what Dad said this morning? He's got to go to a meeting on Friday, and he won't be back in time. I'd go, but Max has a soccer game, and I'll have to take him."

Ellie felt desperate. She couldn't miss the class! Not when Rascal was finally getting the hang of it. What if he forgot everything?

She had a brainstorm as they passed Granddad's on the way home. "Mom, can I ask Granddad to take us?" she asked hopefully.

"That's a good idea." Mom nodded. "Let's go and see if he's home."

Granddad was delighted with the idea, and said he'd been meaning to ask

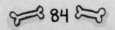

if he could come and watch a lesson. He promised to pick them up in plenty of time on Friday.

Ellie told Granddad all about her problems with Amelia, and about Jack and Hugo on their way to the class. "I'd never seen such a big dog. You just won't believe the size of him," she said. "About fifty times bigger than Rascal."

Granddad nodded. "I love Great Danes. They're so gentle."

But even though he had been warned, Granddad still gasped at the sight of Hugo.

"Has he gotten bigger since Tuesday?" Ellie asked Jack, laughing.

Jack nodded. "He's growing so fast. But he still wants to sit on my lap like he's tiny! Is this your granddad?"

"Nice to meet you, Jack. I'm looking forward to seeing what you both can do," Granddad told them, sitting down at the side of the hall. "Don't look so worried, Ellie. Rascal's going to be great." He beckoned her close and whispered, "Which one's that girl Amelia you told me about?"

Ellie pointed to Amelia and Goldie, and

My Naughty Little Puppy

Granddad nodded. "Mmm. Looks snobby. And that spaniel's nervous—look at her ears twitching. Rascal may be naughty, but he knows he's loved, and that's important. Don't let her bother you." He folded his arms firmly.

Somehow, having Granddad there to watch—smiling as they walked to heel down the hall, and giving her an approving nod when Rascal sat on the first try—was really encouraging.

My Naughty Little Puppy

Ellie gave him a hug at the end of the class. "You were a huge help," she said. Then she added shyly, "Granddad, I've got this special trick I'm teaching Rascal for the dog show. I put a treat on his nose, and he doesn't eat it until I say he can. Well, that's what's supposed to happen. He hasn't gotten it quite right yet."

Granddad looked thoughtful. "Sounds like it could take a lot of practice."

Ellie sighed. "I know, and there's not much time before the dog show. I just want Rascal to be perfect."

Granddad put his arm around her. "I think perfect is kind of boring, myself."

Chapter Nine

Stage Fright

At the next class, Jo reminded everyone that the show was next Tuesday. This lesson, they were going to go through the tests they'd all be doing.

"Rascal and I will finish last in everything," Ellie muttered to Jack.

Jack shrugged. "Only in the tests that Hugo doesn't get last in. Come on, it'll be fun."

Dad seemed to think so, too. He told Mom about it as soon as they got home.

My Naughty Little Puppy

"You don't need to come and watch.
I don't think it's going to go very well," Ellie
told her worriedly. "I'll be nervous, and I'm
sure that makes Rascal naughtier."

But Mom had other ideas. She
announced at breakfast the next day that
the whole family would go.

"Ellie's been working really hard," she
said when Max tried to protest that he had
soccer practice. "We need to be there
to support her and Rascal."

Ellie had a piece of toast halfway to her
mouth, and it stayed there as she froze in
horror. "But I don't want everyone to come
and watch," she blurted out.

Lila nudged Ellie. "What's up? You're
really pale."

My Naughty Little Puppy

"I think I might be sick," Ellie muttered. "It's going to go horribly wrong and everyone will laugh at me."

Lila looked at her thoughtfully. "I'm sure it'll be okay. Rascal's been so good recently. When was the last time he ate something he shouldn't have?"

Ellie nodded. "I still feel sick, though."

Ellie was giving Rascal a last groom in the yard right before the competition, to make him look perfect. She had spent the whole weekend practicing, and hoped Rascal would be on his best behavior.

"There. At least you *look* beautiful," she told him, smoothing his lovely ears.

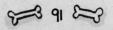

My Naughty Little Puppy

Lila came down the path. "Found you. I got you a present!"

"Me?" Ellie looked surprised.

"You and Rascal. Because you've been so nervous about the show. Go on, open it!"

Ellie tore open the pretty pink paper, and hugged Lila. "A new leash! Oh, Lila, it's awesome! Now he won't have to wear his chewed-up one."

My Naughty Little Puppy

"And a new red headband for you, too.
You can wear it with that red stripy T-shirt,
and then you and Rascal will match."

Ellie tried on the headband, and Lila
nodded approvingly.

"You're the best sister," Ellie told Lila,
hugging her again. "I feel a lot better
already."

There were lots of dogs at the show. Jo had
put her three beginners' groups together to
make it more of a competition. Ellie and Rascal
were last in each section, right after Jack and
Hugo. Waiting was making her nerves even
worse. The judge, a woman named Anne,
looked so serious as she took notes.

But when it was finally Ellie's turn to show off walking to heel, Rascal did it perfectly, even though he was jumpy. Ellie saw Granddad making thumbs-up signs at her, and beamed at him.

After that, Rascal had to let the judge pet him, to show that he was friendly. At least that wasn't something Rascal had a problem with, Ellie thought proudly, as Rascal charmed the judge with little wags of his tail.

But now, as they waited for their next turn, Rascal started to prance around, whining excitedly.

"Take him for a little walk outside if he's getting bored," Jo told Ellie as she saw her trying to calm Rascal down. "I just said the same thing to Jack and Hugo. I'll send someone to call you when it's getting close to your turn to show off 'sit' and 'stay.'"

Ellie nodded gratefully. She knew there was a field and some trees out back, so she headed that way. She could see Jack jogging toward the trees with Hugo, and she set off after them.

"Let's go, Rascal!" she said encouragingly. But Rascal had other ideas.

My Naughty Little Puppy

The hedge that ran around the side of the building was full of interesting smells, and he dug his claws in firmly.

"Rascal, come on," Ellie tried to sound fun and bouncy, but Rascal shook his head hard and suddenly twisted out of his collar, racing away toward the hedge.

Ellie chased after him. She could see his little white tail sticking out of the hedge, and she reached in and grabbed him carefully with both hands.

As she pulled him out, she gasped. Her beautiful, perfectly groomed puppy was absolutely covered in thick, smelly mud.

"Rascal!" Ellie wailed. "What have you done?" She looked back at the building, her eyes wide with horror. Any minute now

My Naughty Little Puppy

she was supposed to show off Rascal doing
his "sit" and "stay." He couldn't possibly go
back in like *this*!

Chapter Ten

The Great Dog Cleanup

"Wow, what happened to him?" Jack said, coming up behind Ellie. Hugo leaned over to sniff the muddy little thing in front of him.

"He ran off and went digging under the hedge. What am I going to do?" Ellie shook her head. "I'll have to take him home. He won't even get his certificate for the end of the course! Oh, Rascal . . ."

"You can't do that." Jack frowned. "Look, can't we sneak him into the

bathroom and wash the mud off?"

Ellie looked at him hopefully. "Could we? I suppose that's the good thing about a really small dog." She took off her jacket and quickly wrapped it around Rascal— with the waterproof outside against his muddy fur. "There's no way we could smuggle Hugo anywhere!"

Jack grinned. "Not unless we walked him along on the other side of an elephant. Come on, Hugo and I will go and stand guard in front of the door to the ladies' room until Jo comes to call us for our turn."

Ellie dashed into the bathroom, carrying her wriggly, whining bundle. She removed the jacket and placed an angry-looking Rascal into a sink.

"Sorry," Ellie told him as she turned on the taps. "Bath time."

Ellie started rinsing off the mud. But it was getting everywhere, and Rascal wasn't helping. He kept trying to jump out of the sink, and he was so slippery!

Ellie looked up in horror as the door opened, but it was only Lila.

"Mom sent me to look for you and I ran into your friend Jack as he was on his way into the hall. He said you were in here. Oh, no! How did Rascal get like that?"

"He found a muddy hedge—you know what he's like. Please, Lila, help me wash him!"

Lila groaned, but she nodded. "I'll hold him. You can't let him get you muddy, too."

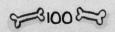

My Naughty Little Puppy

She grabbed hold of Rascal, which left
Ellie free to swoosh the water over him. A lot
of it went onto Lila as well.

"What do you think?" Ellie asked at last.

"He has to be clean." Lila grinned.
"There can't be any more mud on him, since
most of it's on me, and just look at the color
of the water!"

Ellie sighed. It did look as though she'd been trying to make mud soup in the basin, and Lila was covered, too.

"Here, you hold him under the hand dryer, and I'll rinse the sink out." Lila handed her a wet, wriggly Rascal. "Dry your T-shirt, too!"

Rascal seemed to like the warm air from the dryer. He closed his eyes blissfully and stopped struggling.

Ellie put his collar and leash back on. Then she tried to give her muddy sister a hug, without getting too close. "Thanks, Lila!"

"Let's go," Lila said. "It'll be your turn any minute."

Jo was just looking for them as they went back into the main hall. "Ellie, you're on next, okay?"

My Naughty Little Puppy

It seemed as though the emergency bath session had washed away Ellie's butterflies, too! There was no time for nerves now. She and Rascal stood in the middle of the hall, ready to show what they could do.

"Sit!" Ellie smiled as Rascal sat beautifully. "Good boy, Rascal! Down! Down, Rascal!"

Slowly, Rascal lowered his tummy to the ground.

"Stay." Ellie moved a couple of steps backward.

Rascal looked up at Ellie and wriggled after her on his tummy. Ellie tried not to laugh. "Stay."

Rascal laid his nose on his paws.

My Naughty Little Puppy

"Good boy!" Rascal sat up again, and Ellie gave him a treat. She gazed down at him sitting there so nicely. He looked so smart. It was time for his special trick!

She took another treat and balanced it on his nose. Rascal's little tail thumped the ground, but he didn't eat the treat. He watched Ellie, his eyes hopeful.

"Eat it! Good boy, Rascal!" He finally

gobbled down the treat, and Ellie threw her arms around him. She couldn't believe he'd done it!

"That was great, Ellie!" Jo said, and even the judge smiled. "Okay, Rascal was our last dog today, so now we're going to give out certificates to everyone, and we'll hear the winners from our judge, Anne. So, everyone come and stand in a line."

My Naughty Little Puppy

Ellie cuddled Rascal and beamed over at her family. Everyone was clapping.

"Third place, Jack and Hugo!" Anne announced.

Jack gasped.

"Jack's done so well learning to control such a big dog," Jo commented, as she handed Jack a yellow rosette.

My Naughty Little Puppy

"Second goes to Amelia and Goldie."

Amelia didn't look happy as she was given a red rosette. Obviously she'd thought she would come in first.

First place went to a lady with a retriever, from one of the other classes. Ellie knew he had been the best dog in the show, and she certainly hadn't expected to win first prize, but she still felt a little sad. It would have been so nice if Rascal had won *something*.

"And we also have a special award— we don't give this one out every time," Jo said. "It's Most Improved—and this is for Ellie and Rascal. Ellie's worked so hard with Rascal, and Jack Russells aren't easy dogs to train. Well done, you two!"

My Naughty Little Puppy

Ellie and Rascal came to the front, and
Jo handed Ellie a green rosette.

"Oh, Rascal, you little star!" Ellie hugged
him, and clipped the rosette onto his collar.
He was so little that the ribbons trailed on
the ground, and he turned around to try
and nibble them. Ellie couldn't wait to show
Christy. Hopefully, there would still be some
rosette left by the end of school tomorrow.

My Naughty Little Puppy

"Well done, Ellie!" Mom hugged her. "Should we sign up for the next set of classes? You've got three weeks before they start."

"Yes, please! Jack and Hugo are doing them, too."

"Do they teach emergency baths?" Lila whispered. "You'd be good at that."

Back at home, Mom went to make something for a celebration supper. Dad took off his sneakers and frowned at the shoes lined up by the door. "You haven't seen my other slipper, have you?"

"Rascal?" Ellie looked down worriedly as she took off his leash. He stared back at her, wrinkling his nose. His eyes were

sparkling naughtily as he trotted off across the hallway. He burrowed under the shoe rack, one of his favorite hiding places, and came out with the slipper. He held it up to Dad, like the most perfectly trained slipper-fetching dog ever.

"Good boy, Rascal!" Dad said in a surprised voice. "You've done so well today."

Ellie grinned. She decided not to point out the pattern of little teeth marks around the slipper's heel.

Like Granddad said, perfect could be a little bit boring!

WOOF
magazine

Holly Webb

My Naughty Little Puppy

A Home for Rascal

SCHOLASTIC

The Thomas family is finally getting a puppy—and no one is more excited than dog-crazy Ellie! She dreams of a cuddly little pup who will sleep on her bed. But her bossy older brother and sister have other ideas. Will Ellie get her perfect puppy?

Trick treat!

Once your dog has learned to obey the command "stay," you can teach him how to balance a treat on his nose—without munching it! This trains your pooch to listen more attentively.

For this trick, you'll need a packet of treats or biscuits and lots of patience!

1—Tell your dog to sit, and show him the treat. This gets his cooperation!

2—Hold your hand under his chin and keep it there. Use your other hand to gently level his muzzle.

3—Look into his eyes and firmly say "stay." Maintain eye contact and keep repeating this word.

4—Carefully place the treat on his nose. Make him wait for a moment, then say "go." He'll instantly snap it up!

5—Increase the time you make your dog wait during step 4 until he holds it long enough for you to take a picture!